Wash

the
essential
Tolkien

TRIVIA and QUIZ BOOK

the
essential
TOLKIEN

TRIVIA and QUIZ BOOK

A Middle-earth
Miscellany

William MacKay

FALL RIVER PRESS

New York

FALL RIVER PRESS

New York

An Imprint of Sterling Publishing
387 Park Avenue South
New York, NY 10016

© 2012 by Fall River Press
Originally published in 2012 as *Tolkien Trivia: A Middle-earth Miscellany*
The Fell Types are digitally reproduced by Igino Marini.
www.iginomarini.com

ISBN 978-1-4549-1107-4

Distributed in Canada by Sterling Publishing
c/o Canadian Manda Group, 165 Dufferin Street
Toronto, Ontario, Canada M6K 3H6
Distributed in the United Kingdom by GMC Distribution Services
Castle Place, 166 High Street, Lewes, East Sussex, England BN7 1XU
Distributed in Australia by Capricorn Link (Australia) Pty. Ltd.
P.O. Box 704, Windsor, NSW 2756, Australia

For information about custom editions, special sales, and premium and
corporate purchases, please contact Sterling Special Sales at 800-805-5489
or specialsales@sterlingpublishing.com.

Manufactured in the United States of America

2 4 6 8 10 9 7 5 3 1

The author wishes to thank all those who have helped him in the conception, writing, and production of this little book, especially Maureen Slattery, Rick Campbell, Michelle Faulkner, Theresa Thompson, and my editor Chris Barsanti. And, of course, like every other researcher in Middle-earth lore, I owe a great debt to all those who have labored before me in these bright fields. Such ardent, merry scholars are, of course, too numerous to name.

This book is dedicated to my sweet niece Hilary Pease, my friend Keith Dueker, and my dear sister Ellen MacKay Pease.

CONTENTS

INTRODUCTION

J. R. R. Tolkien is a trivia quiz writer's dream. Others write novels or poems; the author of *The Hobbit* and *The Lord of the Rings* devoted decades to weaving together a consistent, detailed Middle-earth mythology. With other fiction, we merely follow the plots; with Tolkien, we acclimate ourselves in a resonant new cosmos where characters and species intermingle and resurface over centuries.

If Tolkien's works are fitting subjects for quiz books and video games, the reflective Oxford academic himself seems an unlikely candidate to be a bestselling author and, posthumously, the center of a multibillion-dollar book and movie franchise. More interested in Old Norse etymologies than in modern day self-promotion, he had little taste for fame and even less for the cult-figure status that the counterculture movement bestowed upon him late in life. The scholar who composed a 2,000-page translation and commentary on *Beowulf* spent almost no time hawking his fiction manuscripts. In fact, it entailed some persuasion for him to even submit *The Hobbit* to a publishing company.

My introduction to Tolkien preceded the full onslaught of his fame. My interest was first awakened, as I remember, by an early appreciation of his writings by Guy Davenport, who had studied under him as a Rhodes Scholar at Oxford. Soon thereafter, I encountered two longtime friends of Tolkien at my own college, Drew University. His close associate Owen Barfield and his former student James H. Pain both presented *The Lord of the Rings* author as a major writer and erudite thinker whose works deserve meticulous attention.

That, of course, does not mean that Tolkien's writings are not also great fun. Indeed, his epic fantasy exists today only because he so enjoyed writing it. Even when he most doubted its commercial viability, he freely confessed that for him, these evocative tales possessed endless fascination. But the entertaining qualities of Tolkien's work do not demand the author's advanced credentials to appreciate. Thus, for example, it might enhance our understanding of Smaug to know that his creation owes something to both the "old night-scather" of *Beowulf* and Fafnir in Norse versions of the Sigurd story, we can take pleasure in this "most specially greedy, strong and wicked worm" without academic preparation.

As Tom Shippey noted, perhaps Tolkien's major achievement was to have opened up the fairy-tale for the contemporary imagination. The success of that project can be measured by our easy acceptance of the novels' incongruities; for instance, Bilbo searches for a match, although they weren't invented until 1837, and displays a recurring obsession with fried eggs and bacon, a very contemporary British conception of breakfast. In the best sense, his work is timeless, projecting both forward and back. It should not surprise us that Tolkien also possessed a clear sense that ancient folkways had survived in the English countryside and, indeed, on both sides of the Atlantic. Davenport, my first guide to the author, recognized this clearly. In his obituary, he noted that Tolkien had earnestly picked the brain of an old Oxford classmate for minutiae about the habits and customs of rural Kentuckians. Then Davenport himself wondered, "Who can say why the Orcs have Hittite names? Who has noticed that Gandalf is Sherlock Holmes in a wizard's hat?"

Ultimately, all Tolkien readers are like Bilbo and Frodo, returning home from our quest with all the lessons we care to keep. I hope that in some small way, this little packet will help keep you happy until the end of your days and that those will be extraordinarily long.

William MacKay
FEBRUARY 2012

THE
MYTHMAKER

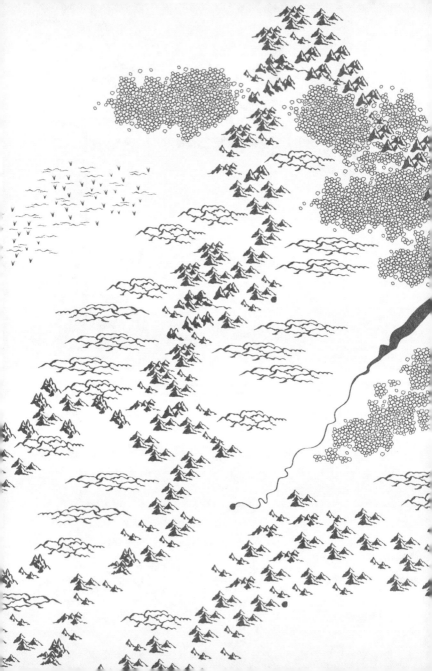

Q: What does the name Tolkien mean?

Q: What Tolkien pseudonym plays on the etymology of his family name?

Q: What was J. R. R. Tolkien's full name?

Q: He was born in:
   a. London
   b. Birmingham
   c. Rhodesia
   d. Oxford
   e. South Africa

A: Etymologically, the word Tolkien is believed to be of German origin. *Toll-kühn* means "foolishly brave" or "stupidly clever."

A: Tolkien wrote sometimes under the pen name of "Oxymore," the French word for "oxymoron."

A: John Ronald Reuel Tolkien. As a child he was called Ronald.

A: e. South Africa. J. R. R. Tolkien was born in Bloemfontein, South Africa, on January 3, 1892. Arthur Reuel Tolkien, his father, had migrated to Africa because he had hoped that the move would advance his career in banking.

Q: Tolkien's memories of his early childhood were scattered, yet vivid. He recalled being bitten by a giant, hairy spider in the family garden but had no recollection at all of an episode that terrorized his family. What was the incident that Tolkien didn't remember?

Q: Not long after J. R. R.'s fourth birthday, something happened that changed his life. What was it?

Q: At what age did Tolkien become an orphan?

A: When he was a baby, he was "kidnapped" by a domestic worker. When matters were eventually sorted out, a different interpretation emerged: Isaak, the servant, had merely borrowed baby Ronald to show to his own family and neighbors. He was neither prosecuted nor punished, and life returned to normal.

A: On February 15, 1896, while the rest of the family was in England, Arthur Tolkien died in Bloemfontein. Tolkien's widowed mother decided not to return to Africa, and she moved the family to the Birmingham area in the West Midlands.

A: Ronald Tolkien was only twelve when Mabel Tolkien, his mother, died in October 1904, leaving him and his younger brother, Hilary, as orphans.

Q: What is Naffarin?

Q: In what illicit activities did Tolkien and his teenage friend, and future wife, Edith Bratt indulge?

A: Naffarin is the name of the first language created by Tolkien himself. (Earlier, he had learned the child languages of Animalic and Nevbosh.) Inspired by Spanish and Latin, Naffarin was an entirely private language. Except for the teenage Tolkien, no one spoke the tongue. Today, Naffarin survives in only one sentence: *"O Naffarínos cutá vu navru cangor luttos ca vúna tiéranar, dana maga tíer ce vru encá vún' farta once ya merúta vúna maxt' amámen."* No one knows what it means.

A: After the sixteen-year-old Tolkien befriended his fellow boarder and orphan, the pair became public pranksters. In Birmingham teashops, they would hurl sugar cubes at passersby. Once they took a secret bicycle ride into the countryside.

Q: On his twenty-first birthday, Tolkien composed a fateful letter. What was the content of the missive, and to whom was it written?

Q: How did Tolkien view World War I?

A: After Tolkien's guardian, Father Francis Morgan, learned of the clandestine cycling trip, he forbade his charge from communicating with Bratt until he turned twenty-one, three years hence! Tolkien obeyed, but he didn't wait one extra minute: At the stroke of midnight, January 3, 1913, he penned a letter to Bratt, asking for her hand. Edith responded that she was engaged to another man, but Tolkien, as persistent as he was patient, quickly convinced her to accept his troth.

A: Preferably from a distance. While thousands of his Oxford compatriots volunteered for the War to End All Wars, the peaceable author lingered at Exeter College, studying the Anglo-Saxon language. Finally, in June 1915, after he had graduated, he joined the Lancashire Fusiliers.

Q: What great battle did he witness?

Q: Tolkien once reveled, "It was like discovering a complete wine cellar filled with bottles of an amazing wine of a kind and flavor never tasted before. It quite intoxicated me." What inspired him so?

Q: According to Tolkien, what comes before the story?

A: Tolkien survived the Somme, where fifty thousand British soldiers were killed or wounded in a single day. He finished the war without a single wound, medal, or promotion. Nevertheless, the courage of common English soldiers left a deep imprint on him for the remainder of his life. Later, he confided that all but one of his friends of that time had died during the Great War.

A: The discovery of a book of Finnish grammar. Throughout his life, Tolkien was delighted by new insights into languages ancient, arcane, or imaginary.

A: More than once he insisted, "To me, a name comes first and the story follows." Tolkien believed that his tales were made to provide a world for the language, rather than the reverse.

Q: How did he earn his living?

Q: What was Tolkien's academic specialty?

A: As a college instructor in language and litera-
    ture. During his career, he held relatively few
    posts. At Leeds, he was a Reader, then professor
    of English language (1920–25). At Oxford, he
    served as Rawlinson and Bosworth Professor
    of Anglo-Saxon (1925–45) and then as Merton
    Professor of English Language and Literature
    (1945–59).

A: Philology, the study of literature and language
    as used in literature. His special area of study
    was the Anglo-Saxon language and its relation
    to Old Norse, Old German, and Gothic.
    Tolkien greatly regretted that a "barbed wire"
    had been placed between the study of literature
    and that of language. In a sense, all his books
    can be viewed as creative attempts to transcend
    that abrasive barrier.

Q: A blank sheet of paper once figured importantly in Tolkien's life. Whose sheet was is it, and what did the author-in-waiting do with the paper?

Q: As a young man, Tolkien was involved in a huge, collective, scholarly enterprise. What was it?

Q: In 1925, Tolkien and E. V. Gordon published their translation of what literary classic?

A: One summer afternoon early in his teaching
   career, Tolkien was marking dull School
   Certificate papers when a single, white sheet—
   "mercifully" left blank by a student—snapped
   him out of his drudgery. On the sheet, he
   penciled one sentence: "In a hole in the ground
   there lived a Hobbit." From that acorn grew a
   towering epic.

A: After World War I, he worked for two years as
   an assistant on the *Oxford Dictionary*. Much
   later in his life, Tolkien contributed to another
   momentous project, the *New Jerusalem Bible*,
   an interdenominational scholarly translation.

A: In that year, this scholarly pair resuscitated
   Sir Gawain and The Green Knight, a long-
   neglected masterpiece of fourteenth-century
   poetry.

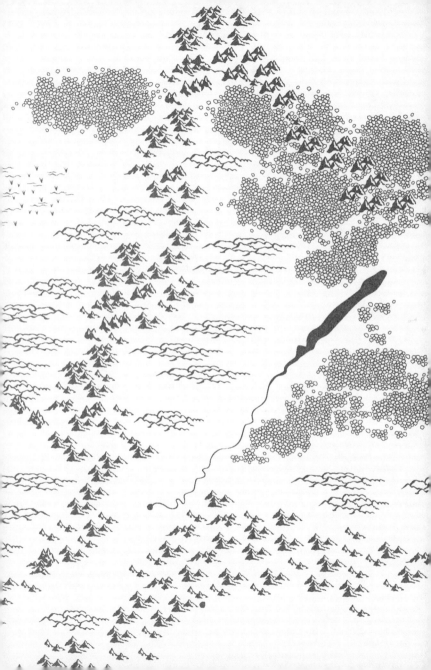

A WORLD OF HOBBITS, ELVES & DWARVES

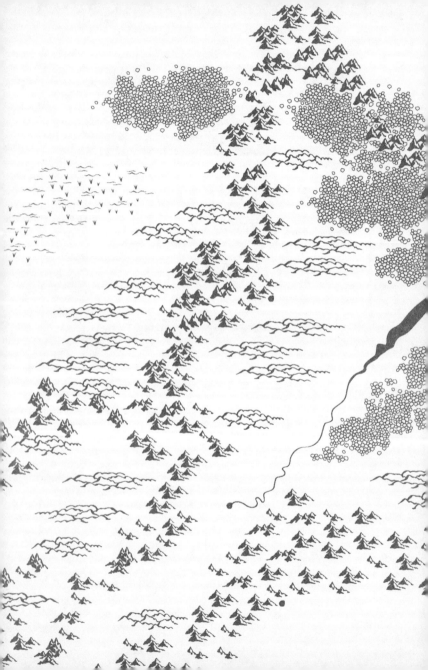

Q: To what nighttime activity does *The Hobbit* owe its origin?

Q: What is the complete title of *The Hobbit*?

Q: When Bilbo Baggins is composing his memoirs, he contemplates giving them a somewhat similar title. What was it?

Q: Was *The Hobbit* well-received by critics? How did it sell?

A: Years before his book was written, Tolkien dispensed snippets of Hobbit history as bedtime stories for his children. Eventually, at the urging of his good friend C. S. Lewis, he gathered the episodes into a book. *The Hobbit* was first published in 1937.

A: *The Hobbit: or There and Back Again*.

A: *There and Back Again, a Hobbit's Holiday*.

A: *The Hobbit* was widely reviewed as a children's book, generally earning high praise for its vividness and originality. In the United States, the book won the prestigious *New York Herald Tribune* award as the best children's book of 1938. Nevertheless, sales for *The Hobbit* on both sides of the Atlantic were modest and remained so until the mid-1960s. For that reason, early editions are now rare and highly sought.

Q: How many years did Tolkien devote to the writing of *The Lord of the Rings*?

Q: Is *The Lord of the Rings* a trilogy?

Q: Name the three volumes of Tolkien's masterpiece.

A: Typing with two fingers, Tolkien completed the twelve hundred printed pages of his great work in fourteen years. Even before these labors, he had been chronicling Middle-earth history privately for more than two decades. *The Lord of the Rings* first brightened bookshelves in 1954–55.

A: Yes and no. As presented by its author, *The Lord of the Rings* is a single work arranged into six books. Tolkien hoped that his opus would be issued in one volume. However, because of cost constraints, it was (and is) published in three volumes.

A: *The Fellowship of the Ring* was the first volume; *The Two Towers*, the second; and *The Return of the King*, the third and final volume.

Q: The author had serious qualms about the title of one of the three volumes. Which of the volumes was it, and what made him worry?

Q: Was the story of Frodo's adventures an instant bestseller?

Q: Did Tolkien ever visit the United States?

A: With some justification, Tolkien feared that *The Return of the King* carried a title that revealed too much of the climatic plot. He had hoped that the third novel would be called *The War of the Ring*.

A: No. At first, bookstore sales of *The Fellowship of the Ring* were steady but unspectacular. It was only after word-of-mouth enthusiasm transformed the book into a campus favorite that sales blossomed. In response to reader requests, Allen & Unwin sped publication of the trilogy's other volumes and increased print runs. All three novels were issued within a fifteen-month period.

A: No. In 1957, Tolkien was scheduled to come to this country to accept honorary degrees from Harvard, Marquette, and several other universities, but the trip was cancelled because of his wife's ill health. Although he lived another sixteen years, he never crossed the Atlantic.

Q: Which of his works did Tolkien consider the most important?

Q: In what year did Tolkien complete *The Silmarillion*?

Q: Which classic was chosen by Modern Library as the No. 1 book of the twentieth century?

A: *The Silmarillion*, his epic history of the First
    Age of Middle-earth.

A: Although he began composing sections of it as
    early as 1913, Tolkien had not yet completed
    The Silmarillion when he died in 1973.
    Fortunately, his son Christopher skillfully
    and lovingly gathered the shards of his father's
    great labor, and *The Silmarillion* was
    published in 1977.

A: James Joyce's *Ulysses*. (Gotcha!) The Modern
    Library panel adjudged the 1922 classic as
    the premier book of the past hundred years.
    The Lord of the Rings was not even listed
    among the top one hundred titles! However,
    this troubling oversight has been corrected
    by other Best of the Century polls. In fact,
    Tolkien's trilogy headed lists in several reader
    surveys, including the BBC/Waterstones and a
    Folio Society poll.

Q: Why does Rayner Unwin deserve a footnote in
literary history?

Q: How did Unwin earn a second footnote in
literary history?

A: Soon after publisher Stanley Unwin first received the typescript of *The Hobbit*, he matter-of-factly passed it along to his eleven-year-old son, Rayner Unwin, for review. Master Unwin's report, though not unequivocal, was sufficiently enthusiastic to convince his father to publish this unknown author. Tolkien, to his credit, did not take umbrage at Rayner's pre-teen suggestions. In fact, he called him "a very reliable critic."

A: In 1950, Unwin the Younger, by now a partner in his father's firm, heard that a reader at George Allen & Unwin had read and rejected a new submission by J. R. R. Tolkien: *The Lord of the Rings*! Taking the manuscript in hand, Rayner cabled his father that *The Lord of the Rings* was a work of genius, although publishing it might lose the firm a thousand pounds (approximately three thousand dollars). Cabling back, Sir Stanley Unwin opined that a work of genius might be worth a thousand pounds. Regrettably, Unwin never witnessed the full impact of the Tolkien renaissance; he died in 2000.

Q: Speaking of the price of genius, how much would a set of first editions of *The Hobbit* and *The Lord of the Rings* fetch today?

Q: Is J. K. Rowling a Tolkien fan?

Q: According to his friend W. H. Auden, who influenced J. R. R. Tolkien?

A: To obtain fine copies in dust jackets of the original Allen & Unwin first editions of *The Hobbit* and the trilogy, one could expect to pay approximately thirty-five thousand dollars.

A: Yes. Though not an avid reader of fantasy, Rowling "loves" *The Hobbit*, which she first read after she had begun her Harry Potter books. She read *The Lord of the Rings* trilogy when she was a teenager. Like most authors, Rowling discourages comparisons with past masters. Nevertheless, she has expressed admiration for Tolkien's creation of a whole mythology, but adds, "On the other hand, I think I have better jokes."

A: No one at all: "You might as well as try to influence a Bandersnatch." Auden was not complaining. He described *The Hobbit* as one of the best children's stories of the twentieth century. (A Bandersnatch, in case you have forgotten, is a fictional creature in Lewis Carroll's *Through the Looking-Glass* and "The Hunting of the Snark.")

Q: Which renowned English poet attended Tolkien's lectures as an undergraduate and never forgot the master's rendition of *Beowulf*?

Q: With what event do the years in Middle-earth begin to be numbered?

Q: How does the Age of the Trees end?

Q: In what year did critic Philip Toynbee predict that the Tolkien craze would soon be over?

Q: What are the three Elder races?

A: Long after both were famous, W. H. Auden told his former professor that he had recited the Old English epic with the voice of Gandalf.

A: The Count of Time began with the creation of the Two Trees; however, it might be argued that years began to be recorded only after the Valar created the Sun and the Moon, thus beginning the First Age. With the rising of that sun, Men awoke and years began to be tallied.

A: The destruction of the Two Trees by Morgoth and Ungoliant brought a violent conclusion to that primordial time.

A: 1961. Toynbee, who died in 1981, did not live to see his dark expectations fulfilled.

A: Dwarves, Elves, and Men.

Q: What is the difference between "dwarve" and "dwarf"?

Q: Why are Dwarves so rich?

Q: What is Mithril?

A: Dwarves (singular: Dwarve) reside in Middle-earth. Dwarfs (singular: dwarf) are the "little people" who share the real earth with not-so-small humans.

A: Almost always, Dwarves lived underground, preferably in or under a mountain. These powerful and energetic creatures constructed subterranean cities with vast chambers and intricate passageways. While tunneling, the Dwarves discovered huge caches of gold, silver, jewels, and Mithril.

A: Mithril, also called truesilver and silver-steel, is a metal with extraordinary properties. It could be forged into a light yet steel-like substance; could be polished like glass; and, though it possessed the shine of silver, it would not tarnish. Not surprisingly, Sauron craved the stuff and hoarded the Mithril gathered by his all-too-faithful goblins and Orcs. Still, a few Mithril items remained, such as Bilbo's Dwarve mail and Nenya, the Elven Ring.

Q: Are the Inklings Dwarves or Elves?

Q: Whose tongue is called "hideous and foul and utterly unlike the languages of the Quendi"?

Q: What is the derivation of *Hobbits*?

A: Neither. The Inklings were a circle of talented Oxford-based writers that included Tolkien, C. S. Lewis, Charles Williams, Owen Barfield, and Neville Coghill. During the Thirties and Forties, this informal group met twice weekly over beer and manuscripts to review each other's writings and the state of the culture. (Despite reports to the contrary, Dorothy Sayers was never a member of the Inklings. Indeed, according to Lewis, she probably did not even know of the circle's existence.)

A: That of the Orcs, of course.

A: The word "Hobbits" is a form of "Holbytlan," a word for "hole-dwellers" that Tolkien speculated, on somewhat shaky grounds, might be a derived form of an Old English word such as *"Holbytla."*

Q: Was Tolkien the first historian of Hobbits?

Q: Does the narrator of *The Hobbit* prefer happy or unhappy stories?

Q: In what land do Hobbits live?

A: Perhaps not. In 1979, Tolkien's student and fellow philologist Robert Burchfield paid tribute to "the plain-looking, waist-coated man with a quicksilver mind" by tracking down one of his mentor's possible sources. Burchfield discovered that an 1895 edition of a mid-nineteenth-century work called *The Denham Tracts* included "Hobbits" in a list of supernatural creatures. However, except for denoting hobbits (erroneously) as "a class of spirits," the account included no information on this frisky species.

A: Like Tolstoy, he knows where a good yarn lies: "Now it is a strange thing, but things that are good and days that are good to spend are soon told about, and not much to listen to; while things that are uncomfortable, palpitating, and even gruesome, may make a good tale, and take a great deal of telling anyway."

A: They live in the Shire.

Q: Where is this land?

Q: Who are smaller, Dwarves or Hobbits?

Q: Why can't Bilbo be mistaken for a Dwarve?

Q: Are Elves tiny?

Q: What sort of footwear do Hobbits favor?

Q: How often do Hobbits eat?

A: Between the river Baranduin (Brandywine) and the Emyn Beraid (Tower Hills).

A: Hobbits, of course. Most of them are shorter than four feet.

A: Like all Hobbits, he has no facial hair.

A: Perhaps in your imagination, but Elves of the Middle-earth are not diminutive gnomes, but tall and graceful creatures.

A: None at all. They have no need for such encumbrances. Their feet grow thick, leathery soles and wooly brown hair.

A: These rotund creatures enjoy six meals a day.

Q: How many floors does a Hobbit-hole in the Hill have? Where are the best rooms?

Q: Which of these Dwarve names don't belong: Kili, Fili, Dori, Nori, Ori, Gloin, Floin, Oin, Bifur, Bofur, Bombur, Dwalin, Balin, Thorin, or Thrór?

Q: After dinner, Hobbits indulge in Pipe-weed. What does this entail?

Q: Gandalf has particular smoking talents. What are they?

A: Only one. The most desirable rooms, the windowed rooms that overlook the garden, are on the left side.

A: Floin and Thrór. The latter was an ancestor of Thorin; the former, a nonexistent apparition.

A: Like J. R. R. Tolkien, Hobbits are inveterate smokers. For millennia, they have loved to light up their clay pipes and inhale fragrant Pipe-weed (*nicotainia*). In fact, in learned circles, it is well-known that Hobbits invented the practice of Pipe-weed smoking. The plants were first cultivated in the Shire, most scholars agree, by Tobold "Old Toby" Hornblower in 1070 Shire Reckoning.

A: Within unfailing accuracy, he can send smaller smoke rings into the larger smoke rings of others. Then, even more miraculously, the smoke ring will turn green and return to hover over the wizard's head.

Q: According to Hobbits, how was golf invented?

Q: If Hobbits had their druthers, how far would they journey?

Q: If an enterprising Hobbit wanted to post a missive to Bilbo Baggins, how would he or she address it?

Q: The Bagginses are highly respected by their Hills neighbors for two reasons. What are the two things that make them so popular?

A: During the ancient Battle of the Green Fields,
    Bullroarer charged the line and decapitated
    goblin-king Golfimbul. The head sailed one
    hundred yards before disappearing down a
    rabbit's hole. In a single shot, the battle was
    won, and the game of golf was invented.

A: Probably no farther than the nearest pub.
    However, some Hobbits such as Bilbo
    and Frodo Baggins have an adventurous,
    Fallohidish tendency.

A: Bilbo Baggins, Esq.
    Bag-End
    Underhill, Hobbiton

A: First, most of them are quite rich. Second,
    they have never had any adventures nor done
    anything unexpected: "You could tell what any
    Baggins would say on any question without the
    bother of asking him."

Q: How old was Bilbo Baggins when he had his first adventure?

Q: Does he welcome it?

Q: During an unexpected party at Bilbo's Hobbit-hole, the Dwarves provide entertainment. Match the musicians with their instruments:

1. Dwalin, Balin	a. drums
2. Bombur	b. clarinets
3. Kili, Fili	c. viols
4. Dori, Nori, Ori	d. harp
5. Thorin	e. fiddles
6. Gloin, Oin	f. flutes
7. Bifur, Bofur	g. none

A: When he leaves his warm, cozy abode, Bilbo
   is about fifty years old, not especially old for
   a Hobbit.

A: On the contrary, he dismisses adventures
   as "nasty, disturbing, uncomfortable things.
   Make you late for dinner!"

A: 1. c. Dwalin, Balin—viols
    2. a. Bombur—drums
    3. e. Kili, Fili—fiddles
    4. f. Dori, Nori, Ori—flutes
    5. d. Thorin—harp
    6. g. Gloin, Oin—none
    7. b. Bifur, Bofur—clarinets.

Q: Who are the youngest of the Dwarves?

Q: What does Bilbo leave behind when he heads out on his adventure?

Q: At some point during their quest, Bilbo and the Dwarves lose their ponies, packages, baggage, tools, and other paraphernalia. What deprives them of their loot?

Q: Who says, "If I say he is a Burglar, a Burglar he is, or will be when the time comes"?

Q: Who says, "Adventures are not all pony-rides in May-sunshine"?

A: Fili and Kili are a half-century younger than any of the others on the treasure hunt.

A: Baggins embarks on his trip without his hat, his walking stick, or money. Even worse, he leaves the Hills with his second breakfast unfinished. Mercifully, Gandalf later retrieves Bilbo's handkerchief, his pipe, and his tobacco.

A: As Bilbo and the Dwarves cross the Misty Mountains, they are overtaken by ravenous goblins. They escape with little more than the clothing on their backs.

A: Gandalf, referring to the relative novice Bilbo.

A: Technically no one. Bilbo never speaks this thought aloud.

Q: Identify the apparently fixated creature who mutters this: "Mutton yesterday, mutton today, and blimey, if it don't look like mutton again tomorrow."

Q: How does Gandalf outwit the Trolls?

Q: Who lives in the Last Homely House?

Q: What region is Bilbo entering that makes him think, "Hmmm! It smells like Elves!"?

A: Like his companions, the Troll speaker had Manflesh on his mind.

A: He distracts them by imitating their voices until dawn breaks, causing these subterranean creatures to transform into stone.

A: The master of the house is the elf-lord Elrond, "as strong as a warrior, as wise as a wizard, as venerable as a king of Dwarves, and as kind as summer."

A: Bilbo, Gandalf, and the thirteen dwarves are just descending into the Elven-dominated secret valley of Rivendell.

Q: What are moon-letters, and what is their importance to the Hobbit treasure hunt?

Q: Bilbo Baggins is on his hands and knees, groping in the dark, when he reaches what is described as "a turning point in his career." What causes the transformation, and how does it affect him?

Q: At that crossroads in his life, what is Baggins pondering?

A: They are a special kind of rune-letters that can be seen only when the moon shines behind them. Some of these hidden messages are even more elusive; they can be read only in the same moon phase and season as they were originally written. If fully understood, the details of the map's moon-letters could reveal secrets about access to the gold hoard.

A: When the Hobbit awakens after being bumped into unconsciousness during the goblin chase, his head is swimming. Crawling sightless in the tunnel, he comes upon the tiny ring that will change his life. It makes little impression: "It did not seem of any particular use at that moment."

A: At this moment of his adventure, as in many others, thoughts of breakfast waft through his thoughts. He imagines himself frying bacon and eggs in his own kitchen at home.

Q: As new editions of *The Hobbit* were issued over the years, Tolkien made several minor changes, most of them to improve style or consistency. For the 1951 release, however, he significantly revised one episode. Can you identify the chapter? Why did he rework it?

Q: While sizing up Baggins and working up an appetite, Gollum proposes a contest. What is it, and why does he choose it?

Q: Answer these riddles:
1. "A box without hinges, key, or lid,/ Yet golden treasure inside is hid."
2. "Alive without breath,/As cold as death;/ Never thirsty, ever drinking,/ All in mail never clinking."
3. "No-legs lay on one-leg, two-legs sat near on three-legs, four-legs got some."

A: Tolkien, who was then at work on *The Lord of the Rings*, rewrote substantial parts of chapter 5, "Riddles in the Dark," to weave its story of Gollum and the Ring into the later events of his trilogy.

A: A game of riddles, chosen because it is the only activity that this lonely creature has ever played.

A: 1. An egg.
   2. A fish.
   3. A fish on a little table; man at table sitting on a stool; the cat has the bones.

Q: Why doesn't Bilbo tell his companions about his acquisition of the magic Ring?

Q: What are Wargs? From where does the name derive?

Q: How are Gandalf, Baggins, and the others saved from the conflagration of the goblins and the wolves?

Q: What is the Hobbit equivalent of "out of the frying pan, into the fire"?

Q: When the Eagles deliver their ritual farewell, only Gandalf knows the correct response. What is it?

A: He is pleased to finally receive credit for his talents, however unearned, from the Dwarves.

A: Wargs are wild wolves. Ever the philologist, Tolkien takes the name directly from Old English.

A: The Lord of the Eagles and the other great birds sweep into the trees to save the imperiled adventurers.

A: "Escaping goblins to be caught by wolves," a proverb that Baggins and his Dwarve companions learned at a high price.

A: "May the wind under your wings bear you where the sun sails and the moon walks."

Q: After the Eagles depart, Gandalf speaks about a quite forbidding, strong man who is a skin-changer and "under no enchantment but his own." Who is this?

Q: At the Enchanted River, one Dwarve falls victim to its magic. Why does this leave a heavy burden on all the travelers?

Q: How many of the Dwarves are captured by the spiders? Who saves them?

Q: When the Dwarves arrive near Laketown, they don't seem exultant. Why are they downcast, and who helps them with their problems?

A: The wizard refers to Beorn, who provides them with lodging for the night.

A: After he slips into the water, Bombur falls into a deep, deep sleep, obliging the other Dwarves to carry him on their backs for several days. Because of their friend's great weight, this becomes an infinitely wearying task.

A: All the Dwarves except Thorin are taken by the giant arachnids. Bilbo, now gaining in stature, comes to their rescue.

A: Their long voyage in barrels leaves the group waterlogged and famished. While many of the Dwarves rest, Bilbo, Fili, Kili, and Thorin go into town for food and supplies.

Q: After days of searching, Bilbo and his short-statured crew find the secret entrance shown on Thorin's map, but one failure threatens to bring down their entire enterprise. What is it, and how is it overcome?

Q: When Bilbo Baggins finally returns to the Hill, he arrives at a most inopportune time. What event makes his appearance so incongruous?

Q: Do Orcs make good dinner companions?

Q: How do Orcs avoid sunburn?

Q: What are female Orcs called?

Q: What is a beryl?

A: No amount of pounding, wedging, or brain-storming allows them to pry the door open. Only remembering the key and offering a riddle can illuminate the path.

A: An auction for the effects of the presumed-deceased Hobbit is nearing its completion.

A: Only if you fancy the idea of *being* dinner. These loathsome creatures are opportunistic cannibals.

A: Because they hate the light of the sun, Orcs cling to their caves and tunnels by day, and fight and cower by night.

A: Nothing, because none has ever been seen.

A: An emerald. Elves love to use them as tokens.

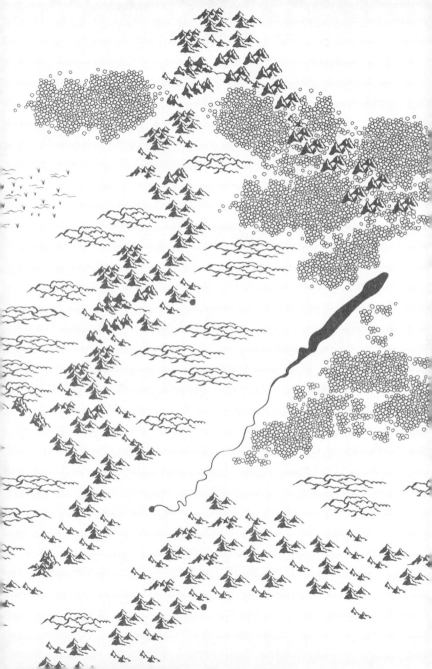

FRODO &
FRIENDS

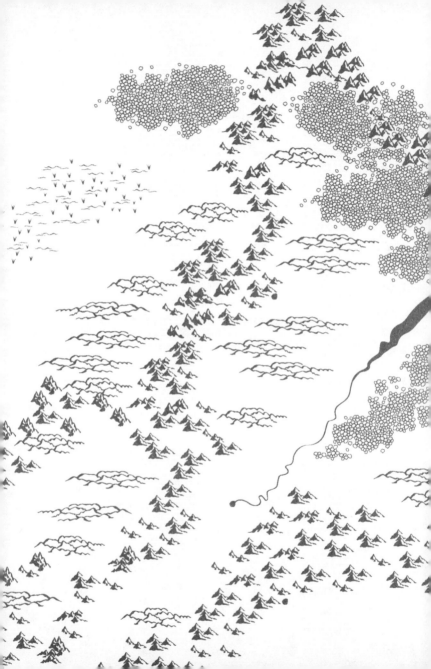

Q: Who gazes "out of the Wild Wood in wonder at their first Dawn"?

Q: Fill in the blanks:
Three Rings for the _____ under the sky,
Seven for the _____ in their halls of stone,
Nine for _____ doomed to die,
One for the _____ _____ on his dark throne
In the Land of _____ where the Shadows lie.
One Ring to rule them all, One Ring to find
them,
One Ring to bring them all and in the darkness
bind them
In the Land of _____ where the Shadows lie.

Q: The lines above appear in several places. Can you name them?

A: The Firstborn, the elder Race of Middle-earth: the Elves.

A: Elven-kings, Dwarf-lords, Mortal Men, Dark Lord, Mordor, Mordor.

A: They appear as the epigraph in all three volumes of *The Lord of the Rings* trilogy: *The Fellowship of the Ring*, *The Two Towers*, and *The Return of the King*. They also achieve a striking display when the Ring itself is placed in fire.

Q: Part of that epigraph derives from a more easily visible inscription. What is that inscription, and where does it first appear?

Q: In what language is this inscription?

Q: At what age does Frodo Baggins become an orphan?

Q: Who adopts Frodo?

Q: Aside from kinship, what does Frodo share with his new guardian?

A: "One Ring to rule them all, One Ring to find them, One Ring to bring them all and in the darkness bind them." These prophetic lines appear on the Ring at the center of Tolkien's epic.

A: It's in pure Black Speech, the language constructed by Sauron in the Dark Years. The inscription, however, is in Elvish script. Black Speech lacks its own written language.

A: When Frodo is only twelve, his mother and father die in a boating accident.

A: His ninety-nine-year-old unmarried cousin, Bilbo Baggins.

A: In addition to being cousins, both Frodo and Bilbo Baggins were born on the same day: September 22.

Q: What are the names of Bilbo Baggins' parents?

Q: On what auspicious day does Frodo receive the magic Ring and Bilbo depart from the Shire?

Q: How many friends and relatives are invited to the gala?

Q: When does Frodo leave Bag End? Where does he go?

Q: On the second day of their journey, our trio notices that they are being followed. Who is trailing them?

A: Gungo Baggins and Belladonna Baggins.

A: Frodo receives the ring on his thirty-third birthday, when he came of age. That eventful day is, of course, also Bilbo Baggins' birthday—his 111th, to be exact.

A: A gross of goodly guests come to the birthday party. In other words, 144 creatures are entertained.

A: On his fiftieth birthday, the hero leaves Bag End and sets out with his friends Peregrin "Pippin" Took and Sam Gamgee for his new home in Buckland.

A: The Black Riders, the dreaded Ringwraiths.

Q: In all, how many Ringwraiths exist?

Q: Who counsels Bilbo to "never laugh at live dragons"?

Q: When Frodo and his little crew take a shortcut to the Brandywine River, they trespass through the mushroom-rich property of which well-known Eastfarthing farmer?

Q: What happens to Frodo, Merry, and Pippin after they fall asleep under an old willow-tree?

Q: How does Bombadil work his magic?

A: There are nine Ringwraiths, or Nazgûl.

A: Bilbo offers himself this very good advice.

A: The quick-witted and ever-vigilant Farmer Maggot.

A: This rather willful willow flings poor Frodo into the river and captures the other Hobbits in its clutches. Only the intervention of a strange, brightly garbed man named Tom Bombadil frees the Hobbits.

A: This grey and bearded creature sings to the testy tree.

Q: When did Tom Bombadil first appear?

Q: Tom Bombadil lives with fair Goldberry, the River-daughter. When is Goldberry's "washing day"?

Q: "I am glad you are here with me, Sam. Here at the end of all things, Sam." Whose words are these, and where are they spoken?

Q: Who are the Prancing Pony's admirers?

A: Long before this genial, blue-jacketed forest spirit saved and entertained the visiting Hobbits, he manifested in "The Adventures of Tom Bombadil," a 1934 poem Tolkien composed to entertain his children. In 1962, Tom appeared again in Tolkien's *The Adventures of Tom Bombadil and Other Verses from the Red Book*.

A: For the yellow-tressed River-daughter, a washing day is any day it rains.

A: Frodo's, on Mount Doom.

A: All those who crave conversation, good ale, and Pipe-weed. The Prancing Pony is a commodious tavern in Bree. Men and Little Folk alike gather there to taste the famous Butterbur brew and exchange stories.

Q: At the inn, Pippin joins the festivities by attempting to tell a story, but Frodo feels compelled to stop him. Why? How does the Hobbit intervene?

Q: Why does the rollicking Frodo suddenly vanish?

Q: Who is Strider?

A: After wooing the crowd with a story about the Mayor of Shire, Pippin launches into an account of Bilbo's grand farewell party. Frodo is worried that Bilbo's disappearance may be revealed, so he decides to intervene. Impetuously, he jumps onto a table and begins to dance and sing.

A: In the excitement of the party, Frodo loses his balance. As he falls from the toppling table, he accidentally slips the magic Ring on his finger and instantly disappears. Not surprisingly, this causes quite a hubbub at the Prancing Pony.

A: Good question. In the merry rooms of the Prancing Pony, this mysterious Ranger is called Strider, but his simple forest garb of greens and browns seems to cloak much secretive wisdom. When he approaches Frodo after the inn incident to offer his assistance, the almost-heroic Hobbit is understandably apprehensive. Only elsewhere is it revealed that he is actually Aragorn II of noble lineage and, by Gandalf's tutelage, the wisest of all living men.

Q: Name the three kinds of Elves.

Q: Which Elves decide to remain in the Mortal Lands rather than sail into the West?

Q: What is the most pervasive Elven language?

Q: Who are the most ancient of all races, "the fathers of the fathers of trees"?

Q: Describe the Ent language.

A: Wood-elves, Grey-elves, and High-elves.

A: The Sindar, also known as Grey-elves.

A: Sindarin, the tongue of the Grey-elves.

A: The Ents, or *Onodrim*, which means "shepherds of the trees." In the almost unfathomable beginnings, before even the Elves roamed, the Ents existed, but they were almost indistinguishable from trees. Soon after the Elves began to speak, the Ents awakened to their nature. They, too, began to speak.

A: Entish is a sonorous language, full of repetitions and cascading adjectives that never seem to move to a conclusion. Pippin thinks that it is an "unhasty language." Tolkien, not without admiration, called it "long-winded."

Q: Are the Ents powerful?

Q: After the Black Riders break into Frodo's house at Crickhollow, they remount their beasts and gallop furiously to a new destination. Where are these hooves headed?

Q: At Weathertop, Frodo can't resist the urge to put on the Ring. What effect does it have?

Q: How many Black Riders attack the Hobbits in the dell below Weathertop?

Q: Who stabs Frodo?

A: No. By the Third Age, the Ents have dwindled like the great trees they once herded. Now, the Ents are considered to be just "a secret in the heart of the forest." Thus, the words of Gandalf: "A thing is about to happen which has not happened since the Elder Days: the Ents are going to wake up and find that they are strong."

A: Not finding Frodo (and the Ring) at Crickhollow, the Black Riders race to the inn at Bree to intercept him. Fortunately, the Hobbits have been forewarned and have already vacated their room when the Ringwraiths arrive to pillage.

A: The Ring-bearer can see the attacking Black Riders clearly, even in the dim of night. Unfortunately, the Ringwraiths can see him, too.

A: Five.

A: The Witch King.

Q: Who drives the Black Riders away from the Last Bridge?

Q: What does the Elf leave as a token at the bridge?

Q: When Frodo and his protectors are ambushed by the Nazgûl near the ford of Bruinen, how does the wounded Hobbit escape?

Q: How do the Black Riders receive their just rewards?

Q: Gondor is one of the two original Realms of Exile of the Second Age. What is the other?

A: Glorfindel.

A: A yellow beryl.

A: He rides to safety on the back of Asfaloth,
    Glorfindel's brave, white steed.

A: Elrond unleashes a white-foamed flood that
    washes away the cursed Ringwraiths and their
    horses.

A: Arnor.

Q: How many years does the Kingdom of Gondor go without a king?

Q: What is the longest and most terrible war in all the recorded ages of Middle-earth?

Q: What causes this conflict?

A: Gondor is monarchless for more than eight hundred years.

A: For savagery and duration, the War of the Great Jewels is a conflict without parallel. For the Elves, the war is disastrous. Morgoth's armies of Orcs and Trolls vanquish all opposition, capturing the High-elven cities of Nargothrond and Gondolin.

A: Melchar of Valinor provokes the war when he steals Fëanor's Silmarilli. Then, after poisoning the Two Trees and thus darkening the Land of the Valar forever, he flees to Mortal Lands and builds the fortress of Thangorodrim to guard his wondrous loot. Enraged and in the folly of his pride, Fëanor vows to pursue Morgoth to the ends of Middle-earth to recover his incomparable Silmarils. Both combatants win allies to their side, and, as the war deepens and widens, sorrow descends on Ennor.

Q: Do all the Silmarilli remain in the hands of Morgoth the Enemy?

Q: Who "sailed out of the mists of the world into the seas of heaven with the Silmaril upon his brow"?

A: No. A single Silmaril is recovered by Beren of the Edain and Lady Lúthien Tinúviel. This noble couple intends to present it as a bride-piece to Luthien's father, Thingol Greyhold. But before the gift can be given, Beren is slain by the Wolf. With her husband dead in her arms, "Tinúviel the elven-fair" decides to accept mortality and die in Middle-earth. As the greatest heirloom of the House of Thingol, the lone Silmaril is passed first to Dior and then to his daughter, Elwing the White. But that is the beginning of another story . . .

A: Eärendil the Mariner. According to this captivating legend, this son of Tuor of the Edain sets sail into the Western Seas on a ship of white beechwood on a mission to the Undying Lands. There, he hopes to enlist help from the Valar for the wars against Morgoth and his cronies.

Q: What happens when he reaches the Shadows?

Q: What part does his wife, Elf-maiden Elwing the White, subsequently play in his mission?

Q: By what other names is Morgoth known?

Q: How does the First Age end?

Q: How do the Elves refer to this epoch?

A: When Eärendil the Mariner approaches the Shadows that bar his passage, his ship is driven back by an irrepressible wind. Three times, this wind of wrath repulses his great craft. Defeated and dejected, he returns to port.

A: Through the power of Ulmo, Elwing comes to her husband at sea, flying to him in the shape of a white seabird. The Silmaril she carries on her breast enables Eärendil to pass the Shadows. Eventually, he reaches the shores of Eldamar. After further journeying, he reaches the Valar and convinces them to send forces to save the Elves and Men of Middle-earth.

A: Before the theft of the Silmarils, Morgoth is known as Melkor. Later, he is called the Enemy, the Dark Lord, and Bauglir.

A: With the destruction of Morgoth.

A: They call this age the Elder Days.

Q: Who says, "Confusticate and bebother these Dwarves"?

Q: Which mighty, traitor wizard kidnaps Gandalf?

Q: Who first speaks the much-quoted aphorism "And he that breaks a thing to find out what it is has left the path of wisdom"?

Q: Like Book One, Book Two of *The Lord of the Rings* begins with a party. In whose honor is this gala held?

Q: What is the longest chapter in *The Lord of the Rings*?

A: These words are spoken not by a certain contemporary American president, but by Bilbo Baggins.

A: Saruman the White, the Chief of the Order of Istari.

A: With these words, Gandalf admonishes Saruman to change his ways. To Saruman's claim that white light can be broken, Gandalf retorts that it then is no longer white.

A: After Elrond nurses Frodo back to health, a feast is held to celebrate the great victory at Bruinen Ford. The guests of honor are, of course, the four Hobbits: Frodo, Merry, Pippin, and Sam.

A: Book Two, chapter 2: "The Council of Elrond."

Q: What is the purpose of the Council of Elrond at Rivendell?

Q: What does the Council conclude?

Q: Who, to his own surprise, volunteers to carry out the Council's wishes?

Q: In addition to Frodo and his three Hobbit companions, who else belongs to the Fellowship of the Ring?

Q: Just before Frodo sets off on his mission to the South, Bilbo Baggins gives him two gifts. Name this pair of useful presents.

A: This great council convenes to discuss ways to frustrate Sauron's plans to dominate the world.

A: Because the Ring can be used only by Sauron and cannot be kept away from his clutching fingers forever, the Council decides that the Ring shall be destroyed in Orodruin.

A: Frodo, the maturing quest hero.

A: Elrond chooses eight companions for the Ring-bearer: Gandalf, Aragorn, Boromir, Legolas, Gimli, Meriadoc (Merry), Peregrin (Pippin), and Samwise.

A: Bilbo presents Frodo with his sword, Sting, and his shirt of Dwarve-mail.

Q: As the Fellowship treks southward, they grow apprehensive that agents of the Enemy are watching them. Who are the interlopers that trouble them?

Q: After the Ring-bearer and his friends are forced to turn in their tracks on the snowy Misty Mountains, they realize that there is only one feasible path to their goal. Where does this path lead them?

Q: Who attacks the Company as they move through the western side of the Misty Mountains?

A: Hawks and crows. Frodo and his companions worry that these hovering and circling birds are spies for Sauron.

A: Through the wretched mines of Moria (Khazad-dûm).

A: Sauron's dreaded Wargs. In addition to these ravenous ogres, an unidentified creature slithers out of the pool and attempts to drag Frodo beneath the water.

Q: How are the Ring-bearer and his companions saved from this onslaught?

Q: While Frodo and the Ring Fellowship are traveling in the ancient Dwarve-realm of Moria, Gandalf finds some interesting reading material. What is it?

Q: In the chamber of Balin's tomb, the Company encounters some unexpected visitors. Who arrives?

Q: After Gandalf uses a spell to lock the door behind them, what happens?

A: They escape into Moria after Gandalf discovers
    the password to open its gates.

A: A chronicle of Balin's expedition to Moria and
    a history of his ill-fated kingdom.

A: A hostile horde of Orcs and Trolls descends
    on the embattled group. During a lull in the
    fighting, the Ring-bearer and his companions
    escape from the tomb chamber via another exit.

A: The Balrog casts a powerful counter-spell. In
    the combined pressure of this magic, the door
    breaks, and the entire chamber collapses,
    blocking the subterranean doorway and
    enabling the Company to escape. (Apparently,
    the counter-spell is invoked wordlessly. Accord-
    ing to Tolkien, the Balrog never speaks.)

Q: When Gandalf battles the Balrog on the bridge, what is this fearsome adversary carrying?

Q: "With a terrible cry the Balrog fell forward, and its shadow plunged down and vanished." What happens next?

Q: Where do Frodo and his companions sleep in the forest of Lórien?

Q: What makes the trees of Lothlórien unlike any others?

Q: Frodo and the Fellowship are allowed to pass into Lórien, but under what two stipulations?

A: The Balrog comes well-armed, carrying a
    multithonged whip of fire and a flaming
    sword.

A: As the Balrog falls into the chasm, he ensnares
    Gandalf with his whip, and the two go tumbling
    down together.

A: In tree platforms. This strategy probably saves
    their lives; while they slumber above, Orcs
    move through the forest below.

A: In the autumn, the leaves on Mallorn trees of
    Lothlórien do not fall; rather, they turn to gold.

A: The Company must proceed blindfolded and
    be accompanied by a pair of guards. After one
    day of stumbling travel, the Lord and Lady of
    Galadhrim grant the Fellowship permission
    to traverse this ancient land with their vision
    unimpeded.

Q: After Lady Galadriel escorts Frodo and Samwise into the hedge-enclosed garden, she shows them something, offers them an opportunity, and issues a warning. What are these three things?

Q: When Samwise looks into the basin, what does he see?

Q: What inspires Frodo to offer Galadriel a gift?

Q: What do the kind Elves of Lórien give to the Company on their departure?

A: For her guests, Lady Galadriel displays a
    wondrous silver basin, which she does not
    allow them to touch. She tell them that when
    this magic receptacle is filled with streamwater,
    it becomes a mirror that reflects past or future
    events. Lady Galadriel invites Frodo and Sam to
    peer into this watery reflector, but she cautions
    them that it is dangerous to chart one's life by
    its wavering visions.

A: He sees trees being cut down all over the Shire.

A: When the Ring-bearer notices Nenya, one of
    the Three Rings, on Lady Galadriel's finger, he
    offers to give her the One Ring. She rejects it.

A: In addition to three swift, unsinkable boats,
    the Elves present them with grey Elven-cloaks,
    several strong ropes, and *lembas*, a miraculous
    little bread that can quickly sate any appetite.

Q: As Frodo and friends sail down the River Anduin, they see a strangely shaped boat. What does the vessel resemble?

Q: Gollum's original name was Sméagol. To what does he owe his new name?

Q: What does Gollum call himself?

Q: As the Company travels down the river, they realize Gollum is following them on a log. This troubles them for two reasons. What are they?

Q: At the Falls of Rauros, Frodo must make a big decision. What is it?

A: The boat (which carries Lord Celeborn and Lady Galadriel) looks like a swan.

A: According to *The Fellowship of the Ring*, "Gollum" was the derisive nickname he earns from friends and relatives for the disturbing guttural sounds he makes involuntarily.

A: Precious.

A: Gollum, of course, is dangerous. Ever since he crossed their path in Moria, this mean-spirited creature has been tracking Frodo and the Fellowship mercilessly. But the Company also worries that Gollum's presence on the river will attract the Orcs who live on the East river-bed.

A: At these great falls on the River Anduin, the Ring-bearer must choose whether to go to the East to Mordor or to the South toward Minas Tirith.

Q: After the Company spends the night on the
western bank of the river, Frodo walks alone
into the forest. What does he seek there?

Q: Why does Boromir follow him into the forest?

Q: How does Frodo end the quarrel?

Q: After Frodo takes off the Ring, he makes a
fateful decision. What is it?

Q: When Sam catches up with Frodo, where is the
Ring-master?

A: The Ring-bearer looks for a lonely place where he can make his decision undisturbed.

A: Boromir tracks down Frodo to convince him to hand over the Ring. However, Boromir's insistent argument that he needs the Ring to defend Gondor doesn't convince Frodo.

A: As their verbal battle threatens to turn physical, Frodo slides the Ring on his finger and runs away.

A: He decides to pursue his quest alone.

A: Attempting to slip away, Frodo is concealed in a boat just launched on the river.

Q: How does *The Fellowship of the Ring* end?

Q: In *The Two Towers*, who captures Meriadoc and Peregrin (Merry and Pippin)?

Q: Who leads the Riders of Rohan?

Q: Beorn, a berserker, is reputed to possess a remarkable transformational skill. What is it?

Q: What savage warning does Beorn leave nailed to a post outside his house?

Q: What is Fram's greatest deed?

A: After paddling off together, Frodo and Samwise find a shelving shore, hide their boat, and then, shouldering their burdens, they set off into the Land of Shadow.

A: Orc soldiers.

A: Éomer, the Third Marshal of Riddermark.

A: It is said that he can reshape himself into a large bear.

A: A goblin's head and a warg-skin.

A: Fram, the son of Frumgar, achieves undying fame by slaying the great Dragon Scatha, which had tormented the Dwarves from his Grey Mountain lair.

Q: What feud later engulfs this hero?

Q: What insult provokes the end of this controversy?

Q: What are the names of the four Ship-kings of Gondor?

Q: "Do not meddle in the affairs of _____ for they are subtle and quick to anger." Fill in the missing word, and identify the speaker.

Q: How does the reign of Eärnil I end?

A: Scatha the Worm has amassed a huge treasure hoard, most of which has been stolen from Dwarves. Having vanquished the dragon, Fram disputes the Dwarves' claims.

A: Fram sends the Dwarves a necklace made of the dragon's teeth and, as if they could miss his point, a taunting note, too. Outraged, the Dwarves kill him.

A: The four kings who preside over the land's great maritime expansion are Tarannon (later known as Falastar); his nephew, Eärnil I; Eärnil I's son, Ciryandil; and his grandson, Ciryaher.

A: Wizards, Gildor Inglorion.

A: In 936, this warrior king is lost at sea.

Q: "Faithless is he that says farewell when the road darkens." Who admonishes whom with these words?

Q: Who says, "I will take the Ring, though I do not know the way"?

Q: Who implores, "Ride, ride to death and the World's ending!"

Q: Who is "the mightiest in skill of word and of hand, more learned than his brothers; his spirit burned as a flame"?

A: Gimli speaks these sage words to Elrond.

A: Frodo Baggins.

A: Éomer.

A: Fëanor.

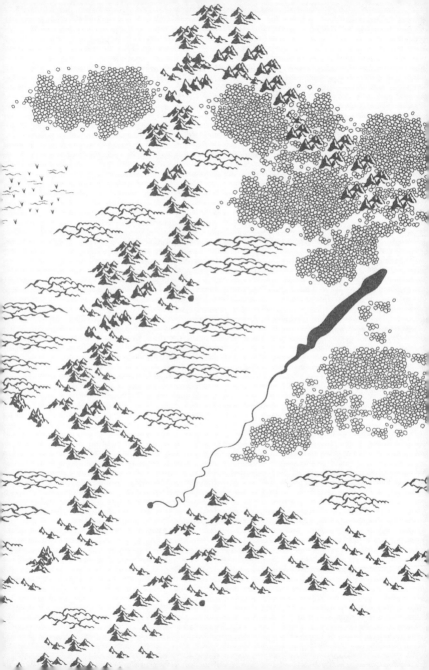

ROADS GO
EVER EVER ON

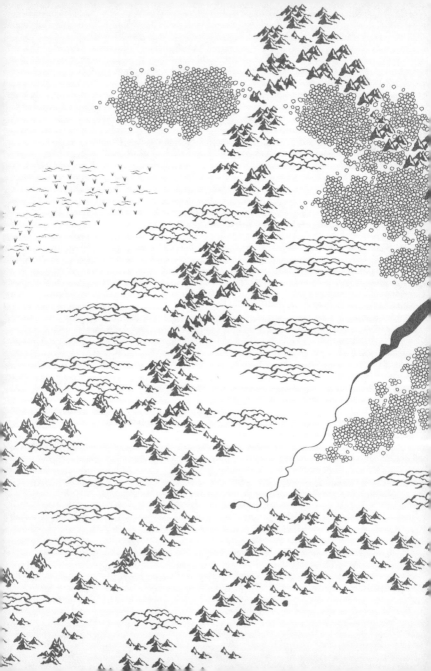

Q: Was Tolkien hostile to the possibility of his books being transformed into movies?

Q: *The Lord of the Rings* film trilogy generated intense worldwide interest. How many people watched the online preview of *The Fellowship of the Ring*, the opening film of the series?

Q: Who directed the films, and where were they shot?

Q: Were these the first movie versions of Tolkien's work?

A: On the contrary, he was hoping that Hollywood would be tempted by his Hobbits and Elves.

A: In its first month, the 90-second teaser of the New Line Cinema film attracted more than a third of a *billion* hits.

A: Peter Jackson. All three were shot simultaneously in New Zealand, Jackson's homeland.

A: No. In 1977, Rankin/Bass produced an animated film based on *The Hobbit* and three years later presented a confusing and truncated cartoon version of *The Return of the King*. Ralph Bakshi was more successful in his attempt to render the stories. Unfortunately, his 1978 animation covers only half the trilogy.

Q: In the early 1970s, a famous director was planning to film *The Lord of the Rings*. Who was he and why did he abandon the project?

Q: Did Tolkien think that filming *The Lord of the Rings* would be easy?

Q: Were the films a box-office hit?

Q: Did the films receive any awards?

A: John Boorman, best known for *Deliverance* and *Point Blank*, made preparations for bringing the trilogy to the screen. Ultimately, the production was terminated because of its soaring costs.

A: Absolutely not. He believed that cramming its narrative into dramatic form would be a major accomplishment. "It would be easier to film *The Odyssey*," he mused.

A: Yes. Together the trilogy movies grossed nearly three billion dollars, making it one of the most successful film series of all time.

A: The entire film trilogy was critically acclaimed, receiving numerous awards, including no fewer than seventeen Oscars. In fact, the final episode, *The Return of the King*, won all eleven Academy Awards for which it was nominated.

Q: When did Peter Jackson first express interest in filming *The Hobbit*?

Q: What are the titles of Jackson's film adaptations of *The Hobbit*?

Q: Two famous film directors were linked to *The Hobbit* before Peter Jackson took over. Name them and describe their connection.

A: As early as 1995. His hopes of making a *Hobbit-Lord of the Rings* trilogy were crushed, however, by problems with production, distribution rights, and other legal issues. In 2006, Jackson resurrected the idea and mapped out *The Hobbit* as a multi-film project.

A: The first of the trilogy is *The Hobbit: An Unexpected Journey*. Its sequel is *The Hobbit: The Desolation of Smaug*. The third film bears the original, full title of Tolkien's book: *The Hobbit: There and Back Again*.

A: As early as 2006, the name of Sam Raimi, of *Spider-Man* and *Evil Dead* fame, was floated in connection with the project. Apparently though, his heart belonged to Spidey and a year later, he withdrew his name from consideration. In April 2008, Guillermo del Toro (*Hellboy*) was hired to direct the *Hobbit* films, only to withdraw two years later, citing the extensive shooting delays. He agreed, however, to continue to co-write the screenplays.

Q: Who plays Bilbo Baggins in the films?

Q: Cate Blanchett was the first actor from
The Lord of the Rings films to be cast in
the films of *The Hobbit*. What makes this
extraordinary?

Q: Tolkien's Middle-earth tales began as children's
bedtime enchantments; then became books and,
in time, movies. Into what other forms have
these numinous quest stories spread?

Q: What did English fantasy novelist Terry Pratchett
(creator of the Discworld series) famously say
about J. R. R. Tolkien?

A: The movies feature not one, but two Bilbos. Martin Freeman plays the young protagonist. Ian Holm, who portrayed Baggins in the first and third installments of *The Lord of the Rings*, returns as the older Bilbo.

A: In *The Lord of the Rings* films, Blanchett played Galadriel, the Elf co-ruler of Lothlórien. Her character does not appear in *The Hobbit* book, but Jackson was so pleased by her performances that he signed her up for a reprise.

A: *The Lord of the Rings* and *The Hobbit* have inspired adaptations in radio series, theater musicals, sound track albums, board games, video games, costumes, comic books, graphic novels, and at least one symphony.

A: "Most modern fantasy just rearranges the furniture in Tolkien's attic."

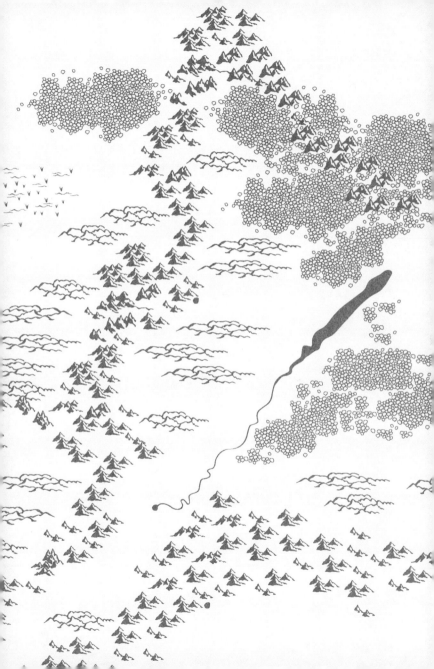

HOBBITOLOGY:
A BRIEF BIBLIOGRAPHY

Carpenter, Humphrey. *J. R. R. Tolkien: A Biography*. New York and Boston: Mariner Books, 2000.

Carpenter, Humphrey, and Tolkien, Christopher. *The Letters of J. R. R. Tolkien*. Boston: Mariner Books, 2000.

Day, David, and Alan Lee. *Tolkien's Ring*. London: Pavilion Books, 2012.

Grotta, Daniel, Greg Hildebrandt, and Tim Hildebrandt. *The Biography of J. R. R. Tolkien: Architect of Middle-earth*. 2nd ed. New York: Running Press, 2001.

Shippey, Tom A. *J. R. R. Tolkien: Author of the Century*. Boston: Houghton Mifflin, 2001.

———. *The Road to Middle Earth: How J. R. R. Tolkien Created a New Mythology*. Boston: Houghton Mifflin, 2003.

Tolkien, J. R. R. *The Hobbit*. Boston: Houghton Mifflin, 1986.

——. *The Lord of the Rings: 50th Anniversary.* 1-vol. ed.
   Boston: Houghton Mifflin, 2005.

——. *The Tolkien Reader.* New York: Del Rey, 1986.

——, Christopher Tolkien, ed. *The Silmarillion.*
   2nd ed. Boston: Houghton Mifflin, 2001.

Tyler, J. E. A. *The Complete Tolkien Companion: Completely
   Revised and Updated.* New York: St. Martin's Griffin,
   2004.

"The Road goes ever on and on
Out from the door where it began.
Now far ahead the Road has gone,
Let others follow it who can!
But I at last with weary feet
Will turn towards the lighted inn,
My evening-rest and sleep to meet."

J. R. R. TOLKIEN
The Lord of the Rings